Mom
I Love You

Mom, I Love You

Hoppy to have you, never feel blue,
my love bounces just for you.

Cheep-cheep, peep-peep, in every way,
I love you, Mama, every day!

Your **purr**-fect love is quite a treat,
with you, my life is so sweet.

Tiny and slow, that's me,

but my love for Mama is bigger than the sea!

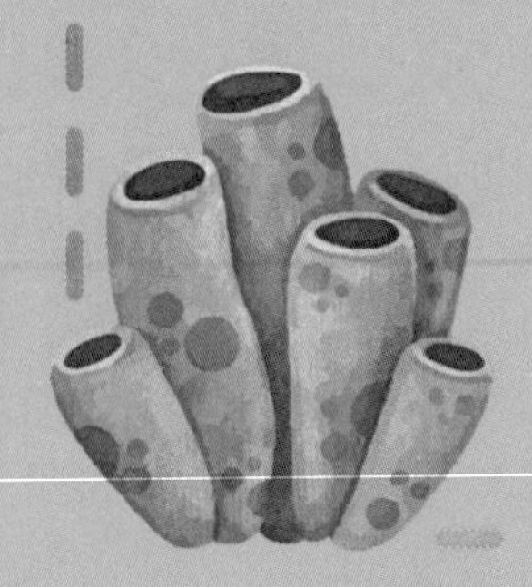

My tiny trunk can't hold all my love for you,

but my trumpet surely can, "Toot toot, I love you!"

With you, life is llama-zingly lovely.
Mama, you mean the world to me.

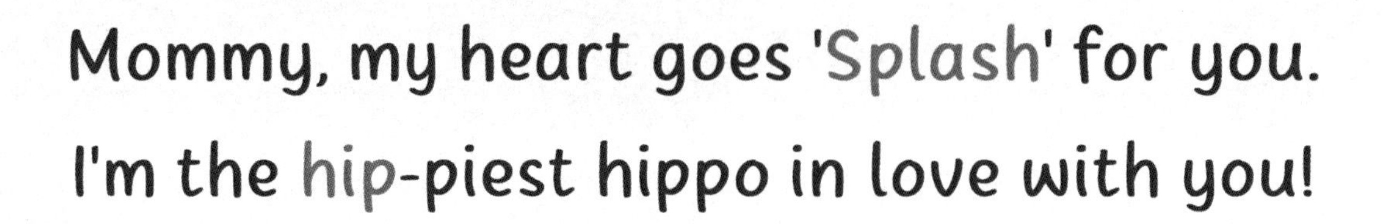

Mommy, my heart goes 'Splash' for you.
I'm the hip-piest hippo in love with you!

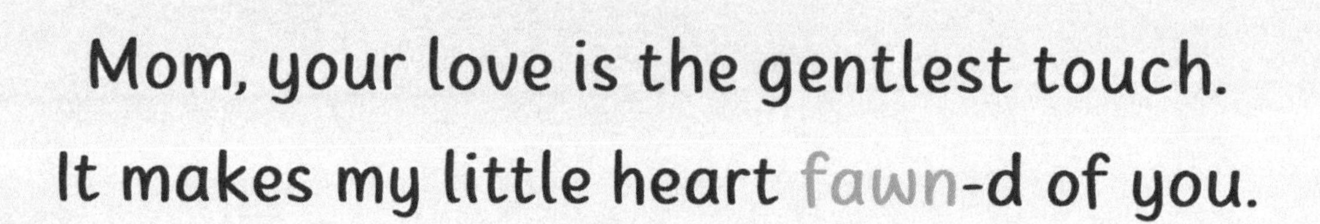

Mom, your love is the gentlest touch.
It makes my little heart fawn-d of you.

My love for you is **paw**-sitively the greatest,
an unbreakable bond, never to be faded.

To my a-peeling mom, I love you more each day,
your love is the sunshine that lights my way.

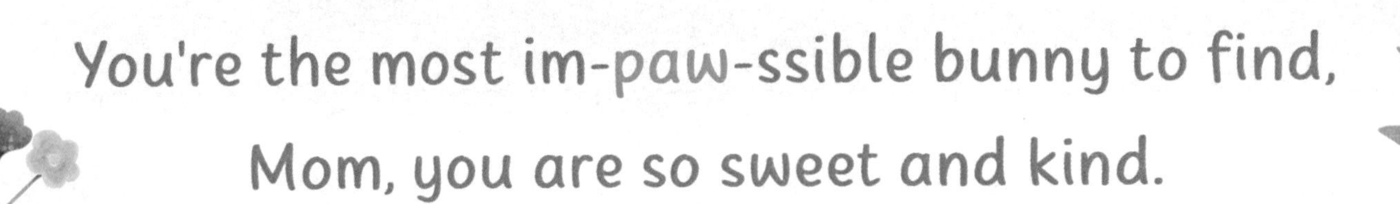

You're the most im-paw-ssible bunny to find,
Mom, you are so sweet and kind.

Your quack is my favorite sound,
it fills my heart with joy all around.

My love for you is as vast as the sea,

I dolphin-itely love you, you're the one for me.

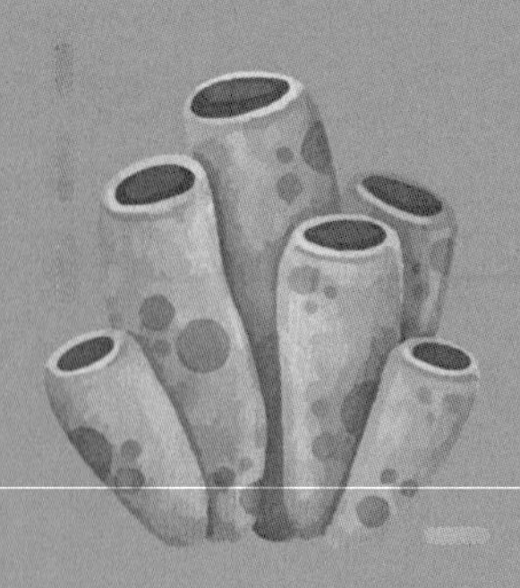

Your lullaby hums are the sweetest tune,
they lull me to sleep beneath your 'spots' and moon!

Stripes may come and stripes may go,
but my love for you, forever will grow.

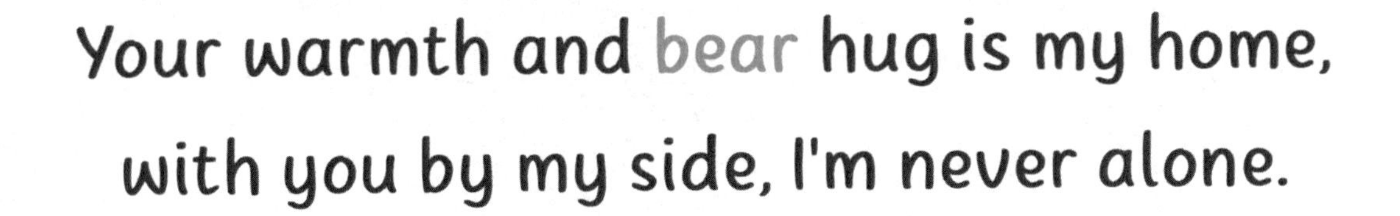

Your warmth and bear hug is my home,
with you by my side, I'm never alone.

Made in the USA
Las Vegas, NV
08 May 2024